The Adventures of

Huckleberry Finn

Adapted by Rob Lloyd Jones

Illustrated by Andy Elkerton

Reading consultant: Alison Kelly

This story is set in the southern states of America around the 1830s, when rich white landowners still used slaves – black men and women forced to work for them by law. These people were bought and sold like animals, and had no rights of their own. Any slave who ran away from his or her 'owner' was hunted down for a reward.

Contents

Chapter 1
Me and Tom Sawyer

This book is all about me, Huckleberry
Finn, and here's something you should
know straight off: I'm only happy when I'm
wearing rags.

I used to wear nothing *but* rags, when I lived
in a barrel in St. Petersburg, on the shore of the
mighty Mississippi River. But for some reason
no one wanted me to sleep in a barrel. A fussy,
wrinkled old woman named Widow Douglas
made me live in her home with her sister Miss
Watson, who was even more fussy and *much*
more wrinkled.

They hugged me so hard I could barely
breathe, and wept over me and called me a
poor lost little orphan.

I don't know why they said that – I wasn't
really an orphan. I had a dad, Pap, but he was
a real mean old beggar and he beat me terribly.

That was when I ran away to live in a barrel.

Widow Douglas had a big old house, where everything was just spick and span. I never saw one speck of dust anywhere among its gloomy halls. She gave me new clothes, but I found them itchy and felt all cramped up.

They rang a bell for supper, and Miss Watson always said prayers before we ate. I did too, even though I never saw much point in praying. Nothing ever came of it, and I told them so.

"Don't talk such nonsense, Huckleberry!" Widow Douglas snapped. "And don't put your feet on the furniture!"

"Sit up straight please!" Miss Watson barked. "Do *try* to behave!"

It was torture!

One night, I sat staring out of my bedroom window, watching the willow branches sway by the river. I felt as if the wind was calling me back to my old life…

Just then, I saw someone hiding among the trees.

Psst, the person hissed.

My heart jumped for joy. It was my old pal Tom Sawyer! Tom and I had been on adventures together before I moved in with Widow Douglas. I could tell from the grin on his face that he was looking for another.

"I'm forming a gang of robbers," Tom declared. "Do you want to join?"

He didn't need to ask twice. Quickly, I scrambled through the window, pulled it shut and dropped to the ground.

We crept across the garden, through stripes of moonlight and shadow. Miss Watson owned several slaves, and one of them, Jim, was sitting against a tree, smoking a pipe. We sneaked past him, and darted into the woods.

Tom's younger brother, Sid, was waiting, and we charged through the forest, hooting and hollering. We chased wild hogs, and fought like pirates with sticks. I felt alive and free again, just like in the good old days.

By the time I got back to the house, I was covered in mud and exhausted, but also grinning from ear to ear.

The smile slipped from my face as I saw that my bedroom window was open. I was sure I had shut it as I sneaked out.

Cautiously, I climbed through. My hand trembled as I lit a candle, and the light skittered around the bedroom walls.

There, in the shadows, was my father!

Chapter 2
Pap

Pap stepped from the gloom. His clothes were rags, and filthy toes poked from the ends of his battered boots. A straggly, greasy beard hung from his flushed face. He looked like an ogre with his staring eyes, which were dark and fierce and glinted in the candlelight.

"Look at you," Pap growled. "Dressed up all nice and tidy."

I wasn't scared. Pap was just a bully. But he was stronger than me, so I had to be careful.

"I need some money," he demanded.

"I'm not giving you anything," I said.

"We'll see about that!"

He grabbed me and dragged me from the house. I thrashed and kicked, but his grip only tightened on my arm. He hurled me into a canoe by the river, and paddled to the opposite shore, where thick woodland rose from the riverbank.

Pap locked me up in a log cabin, and that's where I stayed for several weeks. There seemed no hope of escape – the cabin window was barred and too small to squeeze through, the chimney was too narrow to climb up, and the door was a foot-thick slab of wood.

During the day Pap went out hunting with a shotgun. At night, he moaned and grumbled about his hard life. He beat me a lot too. Most nights I fell asleep covered in bruises.

Then, one day, Pap made a mistake. He left a rusty old saw in the cabin. As soon as he went out, I grabbed the tool and started sawing at the log wall. I worked until blisters burst on my hands, and I'd cut a hole big enough to wriggle through.

It was dark by the time I escaped. I stumbled through the woods, tripping over, cursing and staggering up. Reaching the riverbank, I clambered into Pap's canoe and pushed it out across the water.

I lay on the bottom of the canoe, my heart hammering so loud I feared Pap might hear it in the woods. I was certain he would cry out, or fire his shotgun. But instead everything fell silent, as the current whisked me along the dark and swirling river.

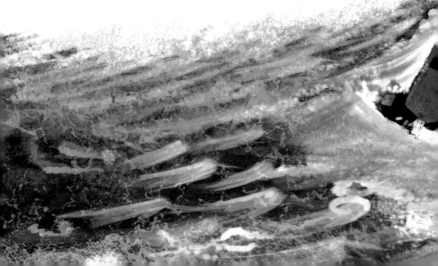

Chapter 3
Jackson's Island

I lay on the bottom of the canoe, staring up at the moon and the shivering stars. Lumps of driftwood thumped the sides of the boat, but otherwise the night was eerily still.

When I finally dared to look up, I saw the dark, humped shape of Jackson's Island rising in the middle of the wide river. Willow trees leaned from the shore, dipping their spindly branches into the water.

Grabbing a branch, I used it to pull the canoe to the shore and then I collapsed onto the riverbank. I was so exhausted that I just lay down to sleep right there in the long, wet grass.

When I woke, the sun was high above me, dazzling my eyes. A cool breeze rustled the long grass. I struggled up and walked further into the island, among the dark, dense woodland.

Each time the branches creaked, I whirled around in fright. I was terrified that Pap would find me.

I kept stopping and listening. But all that I could hear was the wind whispering among the branches, and the frantic hammering of my heart.

Then, ahead, I saw smoke.

I crept closer and crouched behind a bush. A man lay beside a crackling fire, wrapped up in an old horse blanket. Was it Pap?

As the man sat up, a shaft of sunlight caught his face. It was Jim – Miss Watson's slave! I was so relieved that I burst from the bushes and shouted, "Hello Jim!"

Jim sprang up, his eyes wild with fright. Then he dropped to his knees and slapped his hands together like he was praying. "Oh, please don't tell on me!" he cried.

Once Jim had calmed down, we sat beside the fire and he told me his story.

"I ran off, Huck," he said. "Miss Watson was going to sell me to slave traders in New Orleans. If she did, I'd never see my family again. So I sneaked away and paddled across the river holding onto a log. I've been hiding on this island ever since."

Poor Jim was as thin as a stick. All he'd eaten for days were wild strawberries. So the first thing I did was take his fishing line and catch some catfish in the river. We cooked them over the fire and ate and ate. Then, with our bellies full, we sat together by the flames.

"You promise you won't tell on me, Huck?" Jim said, his voice trembling.

I felt guilty. It was against the law to help runaway slaves. But I promised, and so that was that. Besides, there was no way I was going back to Miss Watson and Widow Douglas. Now, Jim and I were runaways together.

Chapter 4
On the river

I've never seen such a storm as the one that woke us the next day. Thunder roared and lightning lit the woods. Rain ripped leaves from the trees, and the wind was so strong we could barely walk five paces before it slapped us back to the ground.

The river rose, flooding Jackson's Island. Splashing through the water, Jim and I made it to the canoe, and set off along the river.

Water snakes and turtles swam beside the boat. Then, as we passed the end of the island, I was amazed to see a small timber house float past. It must have been washed from the bank by the floods, and now it was just bobbing around in the frothing water.

We paddled to it, and climbed in through a window. It was dark inside. As my eyes adjusted to the gloom, I saw an old clothes chest against the wall. And there, beside the chest, lay the body of a man.

"He's dead!" Jim said.

The man had been shot in the back.

"Stay back Huck. Don't look at his face, it's too awful."

Quickly, Jim threw some old rags over the body, hiding the man's face.

I didn't want to see anyway. Instead I swiped a battered straw hat from the chest. It was a perfect fit. We took some supplies too – an old tin lantern, blankets, and some money from the dead man's pocket. All in all, it was a good haul.

Back in the canoe, I asked Jim about the dead man. But he was scared that the man's ghost might haunt us if we spoke about him, bringing us bad luck, so I didn't ask any more. We were going to need all the good luck we could get.

We kept paddling along the river until an old raft made of pine planks came drifting past.

It looked much more comfortable than our cramped old canoe, so we climbed on board and set the canoe adrift.

We had a plan now, too. In some parts of the
country, slavery was banned and Jim would be
free. But it would be a difficult journey. People
hunted runaway slaves for rewards, so it wasn't
safe to travel during the day. Instead, we hid on
the riverbanks and set off again after sunset.

Jim built a little tent on the raft, to keep us
dry in the rain. We caught catfish, swam and
lay on our backs looking up at the stars.

Sometimes we had the whole river to ourselves. Then a huge steamboat would puff past, sparks spurting from its funnels and raining over the river like fireworks.

I tell you, there's no place like a raft. Everywhere else is cramped by comparison. But on a raft, life is free and easy. All in all I was living pretty well.

To be truthful, Jim wasn't as happy as me. Sometimes he sat with his head between his knees. Other nights, he didn't even say a word. I knew he was thinking about his wife and children back in St. Petersburg, and wishing he could be with them again.

"You're the only friend I have Huck," he said with a moan. "But as soon as I get my freedom I'm going to save some money and buy my family out of slavery."

Chapter 5
Royal strangers

One morning, as Jim and I were resting by some cottonwood thickets, strange sounds rang along the riverbank. At first we heard snarls and barks, coming closer. Then there were awful loud screams and shouts and calls for help.

Two men raced along the bank. They were being chased by dogs.

"Save our lives!" one of them shrieked.

"We're innocent men!" the other wailed.

They jumped on board the raft, and we pushed off onto the river. One of the men was bald, with wispy white whiskers and dark, beady eyes like a shark. The other was younger, although his face looked as worn out as the battered old carpet bag he carried.

I asked them what happened, and they groaned. "We were run out of town!" one of the men exclaimed. "Us!"

"Who are you?" Jim asked.

I saw one of the men throw the other a quick, sly glance. "Well, I suppose we can tell you," he said. "I am a duke."

"And I am a king," the other announced. "The King of France."

Jim stared at them, his mouth open in amazement, but I knew that the men were lying. They were con men, people who tricked others out of their money. That was why they were run out of the town. But I couldn't say anything – after all, we were runaways too.

That night, Jim and I stood together at one end of the raft, wishing we'd never helped them. The King and the Duke kept whispering to each other, and chuckling. I knew they were plotting a new trick to swindle money out of people.

Suddenly the Duke bolted up. "We shall stage a show!" he declared.

Both men began prancing around the raft, quoting lines from the plays of William Shakespeare, and acting out elaborate sword fights with sticks.

"Our play will be a certain hit!" the King proclaimed.

I grew more and more worried. What were these rascals planning?

By the time we approached the state of Arkansas, they were ready to perform their play.

We docked the raft near a small town. It was too dangerous for Jim to come with us; someone might turn him in for a reward. So he stayed on the bank, hiding among a grove of cypress trees.

The King and Duke were lucky – there was a small circus camped in the town, so the place was busy. The Duke rented a stage in the courthouse, and the King had some posters printed. We pinned them up all over town.

FOR ONE NIGHT ONLY!

WILLIAM SHAKESPEARE'S THRILLING SWORD FIGHTS, SPEECHES AND LOVE SCENES!

That night, the courthouse was so full that we
had to turn people away. As the Duke collected
people's money at the door, a sly grin rose
across his wrinkled face. He leaned close to me
and whispered, "Get ready to run, Huck. Run
as if dogs were after you."

The curtain rose and the King burst onto the stage dressed in the strangest costume I'd ever seen. He was painted like a rainbow, all over his almost naked body. For several minutes he skipped around the stage, reciting lines from Shakespeare's plays.

Then, very suddenly, he ran off – and the stage curtain fell.

It took the crowd a few minutes to realize they had been swindled.

"Is that all there is?" one of them yelled. "Give us our money back!"

"They're just crooks!" someone else shouted.

By then we were already running as fast as we could to the riverbank. We leaped onto the raft, and Jim shoved it out onto the water.

The King and the Duke shook hands and slapped each other on the back. They laughed until their throats ran dry, and then counted their money from the night.

I watched them with a sigh so heavy it seemed to push the raft faster along the river. I realized that I was now very far from home.

Chapter 6
Betrayed!

We had rafted a long way south, and the weather grew warmer. Clumps of feathery moss, like long beards, hung from the trees. At night, fireflies glimmered around us, as if we were floating through stars.

For most of the time, the Duke and King sat together, whispering and muttering. They were looking for a new scam, and soon enough they found one.

At the next village, they pretended to be the long-lost brothers of a dead man, to swindle his poor daughters out of their fortune. But they were chased out of town when the man's real brothers showed up.

After that they just lay around on the raft, cursing everyone in the village.

One night, Jim slid over to me on the raft, and scowled. "They're cheats and frauds, Huck," he said, his voice low. "What are we going to do?"

"I know Jim," I replied. "We've got to give them the slip."

Early the next morning, we stopped at a little village called Pikesville. By then, the Duke and King had both cheered up, which I thought must be bad news. Surely they were planning another scam.

"I shall go into the village alone," the King announced. "I'll see if the villagers have heard yet about our tricks, or if they're still able to be swindled. If I am not back by midday, come and find me."

Well, *that* was a long morning. The Duke was restless and grumpy, and snapped at me over everything I said or did.

When midday came, it was a relief to get off the raft. I couldn't see Jim but, guessing he was hiding on the riverbank, I followed the Duke and set off in search of the King.

We finally found him hunched over a drink in the village's dusty tavern. He looked as if he'd been there all morning, spending the money from his scams.

Of course the Duke was furious, and began to yell curses at the King. The King yelled the curses right back, and suddenly the two of them were fighting, clattering into tables and then wrestling on the floor.

I seized my chance – and fled. I ran like crazy for the river, yelling to Jim as I got close. "Set the raft loose, Jim. We're leaving them here."

There was no answer.

The raft was empty – Jim was gone!

I called louder, praying he was hiding among the bushes. My heart pounded against my rib cage. I was desperate with fear for my friend. Where *was* he?

I spotted a boy on the road to the village, and rushed to him. "Have you seen a slave around here?" I asked breathlessly.

A gap-toothed grin spread across the boy's rosy cheeks. "He's locked up at Silas Phelps's farm," he replied. "He's a runaway slave." His eyes narrowed. "Hey, you haven't been helping him have you?"

There was no point in getting myself into trouble too. If I did, I wouldn't be able to help Jim. "No," I lied. "I wanted to claim the reward for catching him."

"Well you're too late," the boy said. "An old man in the village turned him in for forty dollars. He's been in the tavern ever since, spending his reward."

I wanted to scream with rage. The boy meant the King – that old swindler was behind this. After all the help we had given him, he'd sold Jim back into slavery.

I walked back to the raft in a daze. I thought of all the adventures Jim and I had had together. Then I pictured him locked in chains, working again as a slave…

I had to save him.

So I started thinking up a plan.

Chapter 7
The rescue plan

Everything was silent and still when I crept to the Phelps's farm, where I'd been told Jim was being kept in chains. I could hear the flies buzzing in the air.

The farm had a big log house for the family, and small wooden cabins for the slaves. I could see several slaves working in the cotton fields, struggling under the weight of the loaded baskets on their backs.

But I couldn't see Jim. I wanted to cry out for him, but couldn't risk being caught.

I jumped the fence and darted for the house, my heart pounding as fast as my feet. Then... disaster!

A pack of dogs charged from the house. They surrounded me, howling and snarling and showing their vicious teeth. I thought they might eat me for lunch, but now the farmer's wife ran from the kitchen, yelling at the beasts. She whacked one of them on the nose with a rolling pin, and they all scampered off.

I feared I was caught, but the woman's face lit up with a smile. "It's you!" she cried.

I had no idea who she thought I was, but I nodded and smiled back.

Tears of joy ran down the woman's cheeks, and she grabbed me in a tight hug. "We expected you two days ago, Tom," she said. "Was your boat delayed?"

Cold sweat slid down by back. Who was Tom? "Yes ma'am," I said hesitantly.

"Oh, call me Aunt Sally! Look Tom, here comes your Uncle Silas."

The farmer stepped from the house; a man with a face as wrinkled as a walnut. "Who's this?" he asked, squinting.

"Why it's Tom Sawyer!" declared Aunt Sally.

My legs turned to jelly and I almost collapsed to the floor. This was my friend Tom Sawyer's aunt and uncle. What luck! I knew enough about Tom's life to pretend to be him, while I searched the farm for Jim.

Then I heard a steamboat whistle from the river, and panic shot up my spine. What if the real Tom Sawyer was on that boat? I had to get to him first, and warn him about what was going on.

Pretending I'd left my bag at the river, I rushed off. As I raced along the road, a boy approached from the other direction. Sure enough – it was Tom.

He stared at me for a long moment, and then we both burst out laughing. We sat by the roadside and I told him all about my adventures, and how Jim was in trouble.

Tom thought about it for a minute, and then sprang up. "Let's say I'm Sid," he said.

Sid was Tom's younger brother. It was a clever plan, since Aunt Sally didn't seem to know what any of the Sawyer family looked like.

As we walked back to the farm, Tom told me all the news from home. I was sad to hear that Miss Watson had died a few weeks back. Pap was gone too, although no one knew where. He'd disappeared around the same time that I ran off with Jim.

We stopped walking as a crowd came
marching from the village. They were
making all sorts of noise – singing, cheering
and banging tin pans, loud enough to drive
away the Devil. They seemed delighted about
something and, as they came closer, I saw what.
They had two prisoners tied to rails – the King
and the Duke.

The con men were splattered with sticky black tar, and covered with feathers. They must have been caught trying to trick the villagers with one of their scams. I knew that they deserved their punishment but, still, I couldn't help feeling sorry for them. That was a cruel fate for anyone.

Now, though, I had to worry about Jim...

Chapter 8
Break out

Tom's plan worked perfectly. Aunt Sally and Uncle Silas believed that he was Sid, and they were delighted. They hugged him so tight he could barely breathe, and then fed us a huge supper of meatloaf and potatoes.

Throughout the meal, Tom and I kept our eyes peeled for Jim. Then, as we ate, Tom nudged me. We watched a slave carry a plate of food to one of the cabins. The cabin was padlocked, and the slave slid the plate under the door.

"There's someone locked up in that cabin," Tom whispered.

"I reckon it's Jim," I replied.

Tom sighed, disappointed. "Breaking him out of there will be too easy," he muttered.

"What do you mean?"

"A good escape story should be harder," Tom explained. "There should be rope ladders and guards, like in adventure stories."

"I'd rather it wasn't hard, Tom. Why don't we just dig under the door?"

"I suppose that will have to do…"

That night, as soon as Aunt Sally and Uncle Silas were asleep, I sneaked outside and stole two shovels from the shed. Tom was waiting for me at the cabins, with a grin on his face and a sack slung over his shoulder.

"What's that for?" I asked.

"You'll see…"

His eyes sparkled with excitement. He was having fun, but I was just scared.

We got to work, digging under the cabin door. By the time the hole was big enough to wriggle under, our arms ached and our hands were covered in blisters.

It was a struggle to squeeze through, and very dark inside the dingy cabin. The air was musty and stank of stale sweat. "Jim?" I whispered.

The voice that came back was parched and trembling. "H…Huck?"

And there he was, cowering on a broken wooden bed. Jim must have been terrified, but he still managed a smile. "Huck!" he said.

"We're breaking you out, Jim!"

"First you need a disguise," Tom said.

He rustled in his sack and pulled out one of Aunt Sally's nightgowns. "In adventure books, prisoners always wear ladies' clothes to escape."

We didn't argue with Tom; we were just grateful for his help. But he sure had a funny way of doing things.

Jim pulled on the disguise, and we helped him wriggle to freedom under the door. Suddenly, lights flicked on in the Phelps's house.

"Who's there?" a voice bellowed.

It was Uncle Silas – and he had a shotgun.

"Run!" I cried.

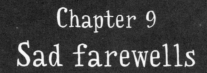

Chapter 9
Sad farewells

Gunshots boomed through the night,
frightening crows from the trees. Bullets
whizzed past us as we fled the farm and raced
for the river.

By the time we reached the raft, we were laughing between gulping, gasping breaths.

"We did it!" I said.

Tom was the happiest of us all – he had a bullet wound in his leg.

I was horrified when I saw the injury. "We have to find a doctor," I said.

"It's only a scratch," Tom insisted. "And now I have a bullet scar, just like the heroes in my books."

"We'd better go, Huck," Jim said, pulling me towards the raft. "The villagers will come hunting for me soon enough."

"Oh don't worry about that," Tom said. "You're a free man, Jim."

Jim looked as confused as I did, but Tom just grinned again. "When Miss Watson died," he explained, "she granted Jim his freedom in her will."

"What?" I cried. "Do you mean that Jim could have been free this whole time? Why didn't you say so?"

"Because it was an adventure!" Tom said.

Like I said, Tom Sawyer had a funny way of doing things.

Jim wasn't angry. In fact, he was so happy that tears streamed down his cheeks.

He hugged me, and then Tom, and then both of us at the same time. "Now I can go back to my family," he said. "What about you, Huck? Will you come back?"

"I can't," I said. "Pap will lock me up again."

The smile fell from Jim's face. When he spoke again, his voice was sad and serious. "Huck, do you remember that dead man we saw in the floating house?"

I shuddered at the memory. "What about him?"

"That was your Pap, Huck. I'm sorry…"

It was dark news, but I refused to let it upset me. Pap was a no-good bully. He wasn't worth my tears. Secretly, though, my heart ached. I wished things had been different between him and me.

I still didn't go back to St. Petersburg with Jim. I knew that the Widow Douglas would adopt me again, and try to civilize me. I'd been there before, and I didn't want to go back. Maybe you've realized by now that I'm not the civilized type.

I'm not the type to stay in one place either. A wind was picking up, and the raft began to pull from the shore. It wanted to get moving again, and so did I.

With a sad smile, I said goodbye to Tom and Jim, and then I set off in search of new adventures.

Mark Twain (1835-1910)

Mark Twain, whose real name was Samuel Langhorne Clemens, was born in 1835 in Missouri, in southern USA. His life was full of adventure – journeying all over America, and working as a river pilot on the Mississippi River. When he began writing novels, he signed his work with the name Mark Twain – an expression used by river pilots to check the depth of the water. He wrote several novels, including *The Adventures of Huckleberry Finn*, which was published in 1884. By the time he died, in 1910, Twain was one of the most famous writers in America.

Designed by Samantha Barrett
Series designer: Russell Punter
Series editor: Lesley Sims
Digital manipulation: John Russell

First published in 2015 by Usborne Publishing Ltd., Usborne House,
83-85 Saffron Hill, London EC1N 8RT, England. www.usborne.com
Copyright © 2015 Usborne Publishing Ltd.